Toot & Puddle

I'll Be Home for Christmas

by
Holly Hobbie

WALKER BOOKS
AND SUBSIDIARIES
LONDON · BOSTON · SYDNEY · AUCKLAND

First published 2001 by Little, Brown and Company, USA

First published in Great Britain 2003 by Walker Books Ltd, 87 Vauxhall Walk, London SE11 5HJ

2 4 6 8 10 9 7 5 3 1

This book has been typeset in Optima, Windsor Light and Poetica

Printed in Singapore

British Library Cataloguing in Publication Data:
a catalogue record for this book is available from the British Library

ISBN 1-84428-001-2

www.walkerbooks.co.uk

To Hope

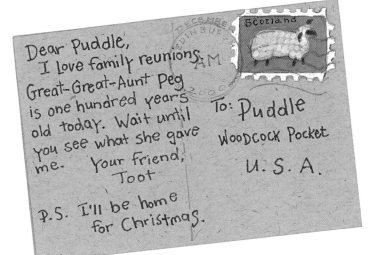

Dear Puddle,
I love family reunions.
Great-Great-Aunt Peg
is one hundred years
old today. Wait until
you see what she gave
me.   Your Friend,
          Toot

P.S. I'll be home
      for Christmas.

Scotland

DECEMBER
EDINBURGH
AM
2000

To: Puddle
Woodcock Pocket
  U. S. A.

"My dear Toot," said the ancient aunt, "this is for you.
It is my lucky nut!"

Back in Woodcock Pocket, Puddle couldn't wait for
Toot any longer. Christmas was only a few days away.
And there was everything to do.

Puddle signed all the cards *Merry Christmas!* *and Puddle*
He would have to wait until Toot returned before he could mail them.

To: puddle@woodcockpocket.com
Subject: Christmas

Puds,

Edinburgh is having a snowstorm. All
flights delayed. But don't decorate the
tree without me. I'm on my way
home...somehow.

Your pal,

Toot

P.S. I'm full of Christmas spirit.

Meanwhile …
at Woodcock Pocket

"Fruitcake is one of Toot's favourite things," said Puddle.

"How many do you think we need?" Tulip asked.

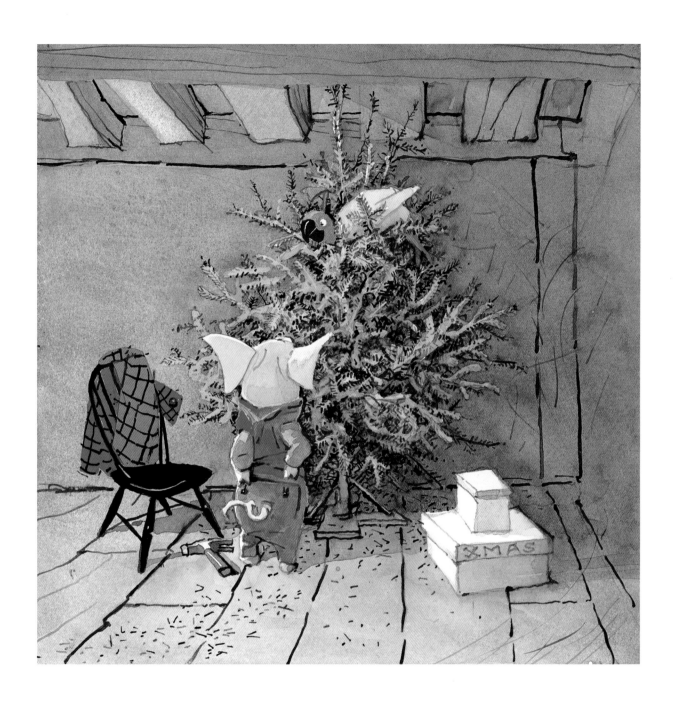

Christmas Eve was only one day away.
"How can Toot possibly get home in time?" Puddle said.
"He has to," said Tulip.

all ... the Way....

WIDE WORLD AIRWAYS

When Toot finally arrived in Boston, it was snowing and very late.
Everything had come to a stop, even trains and buses and taxicabs.
I promised Puddle I'd be home tonight, Toot thought.

Toot hiked far from the city. The night was cold and the snow was deep. He trudged on until, at last, he could go no further.

Toot hugged himself to keep warm. There in his pocket he felt the lucky nut. He'd forgotten all about that special gift. *It's Christmas Eve,* he thought. *I wish I was home in Woodcock Pocket.*

"It's snowing so hard," Puddle said.
"It's beautiful," said Tulip.

"If only Toot were here."

Toot was startled by a tinkling, jingling sound.
As he peered into the dark, he saw a faint light coming
toward him. It twinkled and flickered in the snowy night.

"Where are you headed, laddie?"

"Woodcock Pocket," said Toot. "It's miles and miles from here."

"Climb aboard," the driver said. "I know the way."

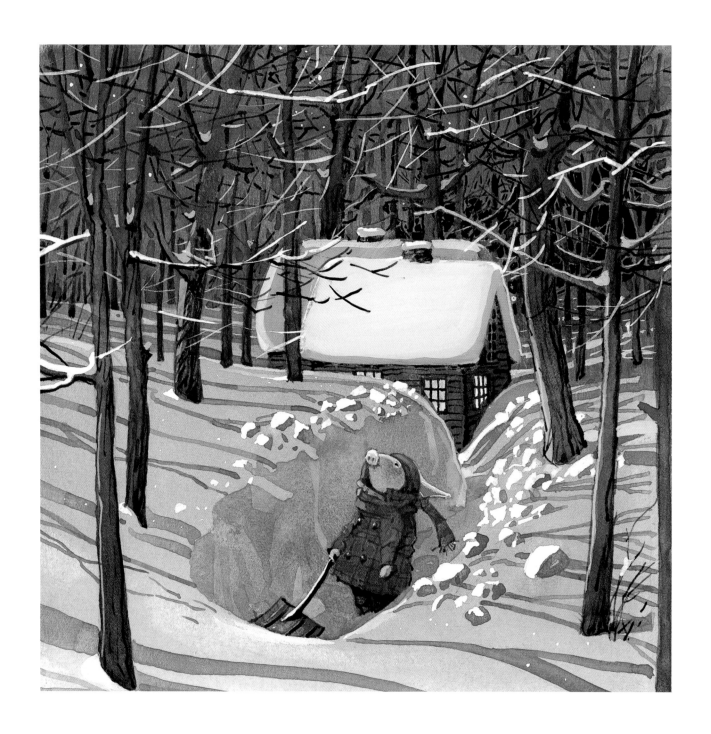

The first snowfall had turned Woodcock Pocket into a sparkling wonderland. Everything was ready. Everything was perfect.
But where was his friend?

Then…
"I'm home!"
"You are! You're finally here!"

Toot told his friends of his adventure and how he finally got
back to Woodcock Pocket.
"I loved the sleigh ride," he said. "It felt like we were flying."
"I wonder who that driver was," said Puddle.

"Let's hang this on the tree," said Toot.
"What is that?" Tulip asked.
"It's beautiful," said Puddle.
"This is Great-Great-Aunt Peg's lucky nut," Toot told them.

It wasn't easy to fall asleep on Christmas Eve.

"Toot," Puddle said, "do you hear a jingling sound?"

Toot listened. "Maybe."

"I think I definitely hear something," said Puddle.

"Then I think we'd better go to sleep," Toot said. "Right away."

Puddle agreed. "I'll count to twenty."

But before Puddle counted to ten, he and his friend were fast asleep.

When they wake up, it will be Christmas.